Tee hee!

Squash the Spider!

For Chris, Ian, Mark,
Richard and Roger.
Great with computers,
useless with spiders!

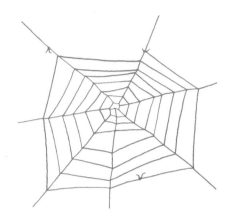

Squash the Spider
A DAVID FICKLING BOOK 0 385 60374 6

Published in Great Britain by David Fickling Books,
a division of Random House Children's Books

This edition published 2003

1 3 5 7 9 10 8 6 4 2

Copyright © Nick Ward, 2003
Illustrations copyright © Nick Ward, 2003

Set in Esprit Book

DAVID FICKLING BOOKS
31 Beaumont Street, Oxford, OX1 2NP
a division of RANDOM HOUSE CHILDREN'S BOOKS
61-63 Uxbridge Rd, London W5 5SA
A division of The Random House Group Ltd.
www.kidsatrandomhouse.co.uk

RANDOM HOUSE AUSTRALIA (PTY) LTD
20 Alfred Street, Milsons Point, Sydney,
New South Wales 2061, Australia

RANDOM HOUSE NEW ZEALAND LTD
18 Poland Road, Glenfield, Auckland 10, New Zealand

RANDOM HOUSE (PTY) LTD
Endulini, 5A Jubilee Road, Parktown 2193, South Africa

THE RANDOM HOUSE GROUP Limited Reg. No. 954009
www.davidficklingbooks.co.uk

A CIP catalogue record for this book is available from the British Library.
Printed and bound in China by Midas Printing Ltd

Squash the Spider!

Nick Ward

David Fickling Books

OXFORD · NEW YORK

High up on the ceiling Squash
the Spider was waiting to pounce!
Billy came in to watch T.V. and
eat his supper.

He settled in front of the telly.

Billy was just about to
take a great big bite out of
his sandwich when . . .

"Yuk!" screamed Billy.
"Mum, **SQUASH the SPIDER!**"

But when Billy's mum rushed in, the spider was gone.

After supper it was Billy's bedtime. "Goodnight Mum," he called. Billy snuggled under his covers and was soon fast asleep.
In a secret hiding place, Squash was already snoring, dreaming up his next trick.

At school the next day, Billy and his friends sat down on the story mat. "Ssh! Let's start with a nice quiet story," whispered the teacher, opening her book. "All about . . ."

A very noisy spider!

"Eek!" squealed the teacher.
"SQUASH the SPIDER!"

Once upon a time in a land far far away, lived a princess. But the ... sad because ... her up ... in a tall ... In a co... a spider sat sp...

Squash jumped!
"Yuk!" cried the whole class.
"Where's he gone?"
But Squash had completely
disappeared!

At lunchtime, Billy was in the
playground with his friends.
"I'm not really scared of spiders,"
he explained. "I was only pretending."

"Me too," said Jo. "Who wants a crisp?"
"What flavour?" asked Billy reaching into the bag.

Jo grabbed Squash. "I'm not scared,"
she said. "Look . . ."
Jo opened her fingers. Squash wriggled
his long spidery legs and . . .

Whizz! He shot straight up Jo's sleeve.

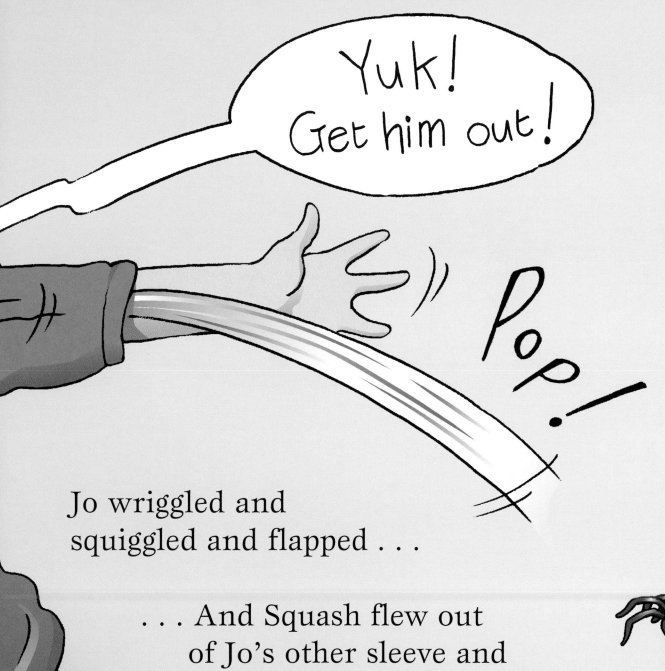

Jo wriggled and squiggled and flapped . . .

. . . And Squash flew out of Jo's other sleeve and tumbled to the ground.

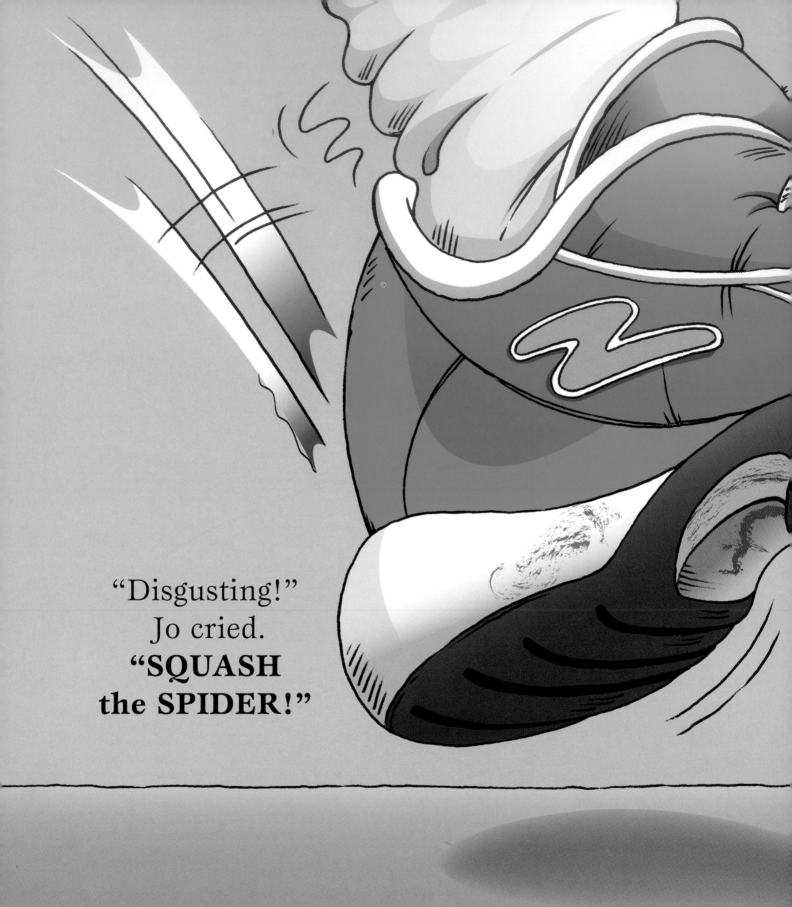

"Disgusting!"
Jo cried.
**"SQUASH
the SPIDER!"**

STO

"Phew! That was close!" gasped Squash on the way home. "But I've learnt my lesson. I will never ever ever scare anyone again!"

"Promise?" asked Billy.

"Promise!" said Squash.

And from that day on, Squash the spider never shouted "Boo!" and never ever scared anyone again.

12

SPIDER LANE

Well, almost never.